DID MY FIRST MOTHER LOVE ME?

A Story for an Adopted Child

With a Special Section for Adoptive Parents

Written by Kathryn Ann Miller

Illustrated by Jami Moffett

Morning Glory Press

Buena Park, California

Library of Congress Cataloging-in-Publication Data
Miller, Kathryn Ann. 1963-
    Did my first mother love me? : a story for an adopted child : with a special
section for adoptive parents / written by Kathryn Ann Miller : illustrated by
Jami Moffett.
        p.   cm.
    Summary: Morgan's adoptive mother reassures her that she is loved by
reading a letter written by her birthmother. Includes a section: "Talking with
your child about adoption."
    ISBN 0-930934-85-7. $12.95 -- ISBN 0-930934-84-9 (pbk.) $5.95
    [1. Adoption--Fiction. 2. Mother and child--Fiction. 3. Letters--Fiction.]
    I. Moffett, Jami. 1952-   ill. II. Title.
PZ7.M622D1 1994
[E]--dc20
                                                                    94-1987
                                                                       CIP
                                                                        AC

MORNING GLORY PRESS
6595 San Haroldo Way, Buena Park, CA 90620-3748
714/828-1998
Printed in the United States of America

To Meghan

Morgan is adopted. She knows her mom and dad love her very much.

Morgan's mom explained long ago that Morgan grew in another mother's tummy. After she was born, mom and dad adopted her.

Sometimes Morgan wonders about her other mother.

"Did my first mother love me?" she asked.

"Of course she did," her mom said.

"Remember that letter she wrote to you?"

"I think so," said Morgan. "Can I hear it again?"

"Yes indeed," her mom said.

She walked over to her desk and pulled out an envelope.

"Here it is," she said. And she began to read:

My dear child,
The day I first learned about you was a
very important day in my life.
I learned I was going to have a baby.
That baby was you.
I could already picture you
growing inside me.
The love I felt for you was so strong.

Days turned into weeks,
   And weeks turned into months.
I felt you move!
I was so excited!

You felt like a tiny tickle
  on the inside of my stomach.
Just a tiny tickle . . . Almost as if
  you were letting me know you were there
    and wanted some attention.

As you grew bigger on the inside,
  I grew much bigger on the outside!
Every day I talked to you,
  sang songs to you,
    and whispered, "I love you."

Each day I thought about
all the wonderful things waiting for you
once you were born.

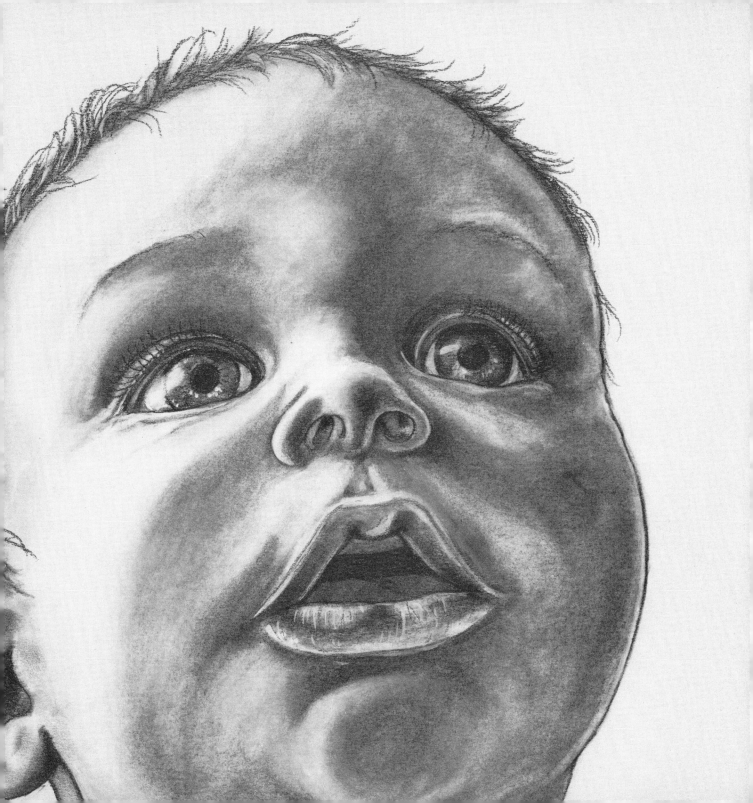

As I counted the days until I could
hold you in my arms,
I told you all the things
I wished for you in your life to come.

I wished for you
    A place where you
        could laugh and feel loved
        by both parents every day.

I wished for you
  A house with a yard
    and maybe a dog
    or two.

I wished for you
    A safe and happy home
    with parents who play with you,
        tickle you, hug you,
        and smile with you.

I wished for you
   To be in a family
   who will give you all
      the love and attention
      you need
      so you grow up happy.

For me, I wished to be the one
to give you all these wonderful things.
Sadly, I knew this one wish
would not come true.

My dearest child,
To your parents
I have given
the precious gift of you.

And in my heart
I know all my wishes for you
have now come true.

Morgan smiled as she snuggled in her mom's arms.

"I'm glad my first mother loves me too," she said.

Talking with Your Child About Adoption

By Jeanne Warren Lindsay, author of *Pregnant Too Soon: Adoption is an Option; Open Adoption: A Caring Option; Parents, Pregnant Teens and the Adoption Option;* and co-author of *Adoption Awareness.*

"Did my first mother love me?" What a perfectly normal question for a child to ask her adoptive mother! The question implies that the child feels secure in her adoptive parents' love. If she didn't, she probably wouldn't feel she could ask about her birthmother.

No matter how well-loved your child is and how satisfied he feels about his adoptive family, he is likely to worry sometimes that his birthfamily didn't care about him. At other times, he may fantasize that these unknown people are movie stars or other well-known persons. If he shares these thoughts with you, don't worry about it—this is normal. This kind of sharing is usually an indication of his trust in you as his *real* family.

As you read this book with your child, perhaps you'll be able to share information about his birthfamily. If yours is an open adoption, your child may be in contact with his birthfamily. That makes the questions easier to answer.

If you adopted your child through the closed adoption process, you may not have a lot of information. You can assure her, however, that birthparents love their children. Her birthparents made an adoption plan because they didn't believe they could provide for her in the way they wished. Her parents probably think of her often. You might say, "I know they would be very proud of you if they could know you now."

When Shall We Talk?

At one time, adoptive parents were actually advised not to talk about their child's adoption with him. Some adoptees were grown before they learned they were not born into their families. An individual in this situation was likely to feel cheated, and to wonder in what other ways his parents had misled, even lied to him.

During the past two decades, adoption has become more and more open. Almost all adoptees today are told about their adoption.

Some adoptive parents wonder when to start talking about adoption with their child. If you think of adoption as second best, something you'd rather the neighbors didn't know, you may find yourself in a dilemma. Your child will know if you consider the subject of adoption distasteful, a topic you'd rather not discuss.

If, however, you truly believe adoption is a normal way of creating a family, you won't find this discussion difficult. Adopting a child is different than giving birth, but it doesn't change the love you feel for your child.

You can discuss adoption with your child when she is very young. It's not a subject you need or want to hide. It's the reason your family is able to be together, and that is *positive*. With this attitude, you can enjoy talking about adoption with her.

Sharon Kaplan Roszia, program director for the Kinship Alliance, points out that how you talk to your child about adoption depends on her age.

Your preschool child is likely to be ready for a basic definition of adoption.

This definition needs to be as simple and concrete as possible.

A possible explanation, according to Ms. Roszia, could be, "Every person starts life in a woman's uterus or womb. A man and a woman start a baby growing there. When the baby is ready, the woman gives birth.

"Sometimes this birthmother is ready to be an every-day mommy. Sometimes she isn't ready because she's going to school or she's too young, or she can't give her baby the things she wants for him. When this happens, she may choose another mommy and daddy to parent her child. This is called adoption, and *adoption is forever.*"

Stress Three Concepts

As you talk with your child about adoption, it's important to stress three concepts: First, your child was born like everyone else. Second, lots of people are adopted, and this is normal and natural. Third, once it's done, adoption is permanent.

You'll find many opportunities to discuss adoption with your child as he develops within your family. Books like this provide a chance for you and your child to read about and discuss adoption issues. Today's adoptive parents are not likely to avoid the subject of adoption. On the contrary, they embrace it as a way to build their family.

It doesn't matter whether mom or dad explains adoption to your child, but the other parent needs to reaffirm the conversation, Ms. Roszia stressed. "If your child asks dad about his adoption in the morning, mom can reinforce dad's comments when she's tucking their child into bed that night," she commented.

Carolyn Hale, adoptive mother of Kasey, 15 months, explained:

We have always talked about adoption to Kasey. He doesn't understand the concept yet, but he's growing up knowing it's all right, that it's a positive thing, being adopted. I think because we're comfortable with adoption, he will be too.

Your child's reaction to his adoption will depend a lot on your attitude. If the parent is nervous about the subject or she makes a big deal of it, the child is less likely to think of adoption as a normal way to have a family.

So speak in a positive way about adoption as soon as your child is able to understand, probably when he's a toddler. When you, as adoptive parents, discuss adoption as an accepted and treasured way of life, your child is likely to accept his adoption in the same positive manner. This early support provides the foundation he needs later when he once again as an adolescent, questions adoption (as adolescents question most aspects of their lives).

"Why Was I Adopted?"

It may be hard for your child to comprehend the concept of adoption. When she is young, it's a fact without a good or bad connotation. When she begins to interact with other children and other people, she will begin to realize she does have a different fam-ily. She may even understand that her family includes another, often intangible and untouchable family. The answer to the question "Why?" now becomes extremely important.

"She made sure you got the very best chance at having a beautiful life."

In order to keep your child's self-esteem intact, you want to approach this "Why?" question with empathy layered with common sense. It's natural for your child to want to know why. Now is the time for you to talk.

You might say, "Your birthmom made an adoption plan for you. She wanted you to have so many things in life she thought you deserved, but she knew she couldn't give them to you at the time she gave birth to you. So she made sure you got the very best chance at having a beautiful life."

Or you could say, "We met your birthmother. She wanted so much for you and made sure that we were able to give it to you. She was sad that she would not be able to be a parent to you, but was glad that she could find secure people who were ready to parent a child and build a family."

There are other ideas you can talk about. "Parenting is a privilege" and "quality of life" are separate concepts, but each is intrinsically connected to the adoption decision. The experience of carrying a child and giving birth is one of the greatest gifts a mother can have. Being able to parent successfully is another one of life's greatest gifts. Not always can these two things be done together. We need to explain this to the adoptee.

The adopted child generally has no say in the adoption decision. He may feel he did not deserve to be in on the decision. He may wonder what was wrong with him, and his self-esteem may suffer. Explaining why the birthparents could not parent at that point in time might be difficult, but your explanation can be more concrete than using the abstract concept of love. All

he knows at this point is that you love him. He has a family.

Learning he has biological roots with another family is the basic need at this time. If you stress that adoption occurs *because* of love, then how is he to believe it won't happen again?

An appropriate answer to the "Why?" might be, "Yes, your birthparents loved you and were very sad they were not ready to become parents. They took good care of your future by planning it as best they could. Finding the best possible family to give you a secure home and happy life was most important to them." This is the message of ***Did My First Mother Love Me?***

Who she is is influenced by you and her family of birth— and her perception of you and of her birthfamily.

Let your child know her birthparents loved her. At the same time, give her concrete reasons that, to the best of your ability, answer her questions. By doing this, you will help her understand an incredibly complex situation in a more tangible way.

It's especially important to be as positive as possible as you talk with your child. She *is* your child, but genetically she has another heritage. She needs not only to feel good about and loved by her "real" family (you), but also by her birthfamily. She's part of both. Who she is is influenced by you *and* by her family of birth—and by her perception of you and of her birthfamily.

Open Adoption

If yours is an open adoption with continuing contact with your child's birthmother, "Did my first mother love me?" is a question with an obvious answer. If his birthmother is part of his life, she surely loves him. In many adoptive families today, the child's birthfamily plays the role of extended family. It takes much of the mystique out of adoption when such a significant part of his life is not kept a secret.

David, father of Evan, 8, said:

I think the openness is much better because we can tell our son in all honesty that he was loved. We can show him the picture of his birthmother holding him, and we can tell him we know his birthmother loved him.

We can even explain why his birthmother didn't feel she should raise Evan herself, but chose us instead. That means a lot to Evan.

Dan and Lisa Green have two adopted children, Joshua, 8, and Rachel, 10, plus Travis, born to them last year. Joshua's birthmother chose the Greens as his adoptive parents while Rachel's adoption was mostly closed. Lisa reported:

We still have open communication with Josh's birthmother. He has met her, and he seldom asks questions. Rachel is more questioning. "Why

*did my birthmother give me away?"
Or she'll say, "What is my other
family like?"*

*We try to give her the information
we have without overkill. We tell her
that her birthmother loved her very
much, but that if she had kept Rachel,
Rachel would not have had a father—
just honest stuff. We don't know if
she has half brothers and sisters, and
we tell her that.*

*Rachel would like more informa-
tion, but her birthmother doesn't
want contact with us at this point.
We've told Rachel she may be able to
meet her sometime but that it's not
possible now. She accepts it.*

The Closed-Open Adoption Continuum

Today some people define open
adoption as the kind of adoption in
which the birthparents and the adoptive parents know each other and have
face to face contact with each other
through the years. Other people consider an adoption open if the adoptive
and birthparents meet only once and
don't exchange names and addresses.

Not too long ago, an adoption was
considered open if the birthmother
wrote a letter to her child when he was
placed with his adoptive family. The
adoptive parents were to give him the
letter when he was 18.

Many adopted children and adolescents today know and have continuing
communication with their birthparents.
For most of these young people, adoption is something known and usually
accepted well.

---

*You can talk about adoption
without waiting for questions.*

Your child, however, may have little
or no contact with his birthparents. His
adoption may be tightly closed, and
you may not know much about his
"first" parents. Questions are hard to
answer when you have very little
information.

You still need to be open, honest,
and positive. You don't want to hide
from your child's questions. In fact, if

the questions don't come, you need to offer information anyway.

You can talk about adoption without waiting for questions. Reading books like this one can start conversations on the subject. Find out about other adopted children in your neighborhood, your church, your child's play group or school. If he has a friend who is also adopted, he may feel more comfortable about his adoptee status.

Carolyn Hale feels this is important:

We have a friend with an adopted child who is two weeks younger than Kasey. We get the two toddlers together as much as possible, and we talk about adoption so it won't be scary for them. Finding other adopted children to be a support group is important. And his parents are our support group.

If you don't have much information, that's what you tell your child. You share what you have, and you explain that you'd like to know more, too, but that you simply don't have any more information.

Most birthparents are loving and caring people who want their child to have a good life, a better life than they can provide at the time they place him for adoption. Even if you have no information, you assume this much. Chances are you have a lot more to share with your child.

Your Feelings Toward Your Child's Birthparents

Some adoptive parents develop an irrational fear of their child's birthparents. Will these first parents come back and take this child away? If you're feeling this fear, think about it. Who made the decision to place this child? His birthparents. Who wanted a better life for this child than they could provide? His birthparents. As a birthparent said, "I love my child. I would never do anything to disrupt his life. I want him to be happy."

What if your child asks at some point, "Can I meet my birthmother?" (assuming the adoption has not been open to face to face contact). If you are in a closed adoption arranged through an agency, check with the agency. What are the chances of contacting your child's birthparents? If the agency says it's absolutely not possible, you can get help elsewhere in searching.

A good way to start looking for search information is to call the American Adoption Congress hotline, 1-800/274-OPEN. They can give you a referral for search help anywhere in the United States.

Generally it's honest to tell your child that he may be able to meet his birthmother sometime, and possibly his birthfather. If you're willing to do so, you can tell him that you will help him search at some point.

Many adoptees say they don't search for their birthparents because they don't want to hurt their adoptive parents. However, looking for one's biological heritage is important to many people, and it does *not* mean these people are looking for replacements for their "real" (adoptive) parents.

Assuring your child that you will support him in any efforts he chooses to make to find his other family will help him feel secure and loved.

Hard Decision for Birthparents

Placing her baby for adoption does not negate the love the birthparent feels for this child. Bonding between mother and child generally begins during pregnancy. Allowing another family to adopt her child is undoubtedly one of the hardest decisions a human being can make, a decision that is likely to cause a lot of grief for the birthparents.

That doesn't mean it was a poor decision. It does mean that placing her child for adoption seemed the best decision at that time.

The adoptive parents and the birthparents all want the best for this child. Adoptive parents who understand this concept generally have nothing to fear from their child's birthparents. Adoption to them and to their child is, indeed, a positive, beautiful experience.

Acknowledgments

I thank those people who with their concise thinking and empathy have proven to be inspirational in a lifetime decision-making process. I especially thank Tim and Michelle Edwards, Kelly McNamara, Leslie McPeak, Marilyn Reed, and Judy Link who have shown time and again how acceptance, love, and generosity of spirit are basic necessities in life.

Kathryn Ann Miller
February, 1994

OTHER BOOKS FROM MORNING GLORY PRESS

OPEN ADOPTION: A Caring Option. A fascinating and sensitive account of the new world of adoption.

PREGNANT TOO SOON: Adoption Is an Option. Young birthmothers tell their stories.

PARENTS, PREGNANT TEENS AND THE ADOPTION OPTION. For all parents who feel alone as their daughter faces too-early pregnancy and the difficult adoption/keeping decision.

ADOPTION AWARENESS: A Guide for Teachers, Nurses, Counselors and Caring Others. Guide for supporting adoption alternative in crisis pregnancy.

SURVIVING TEEN PREGNANCY: Choices, Dreams, and Decisions by Shirley Arthur. For all pregnant teens—help with decisions, moving on toward goals.

TEEN DADS: Rights, Responsibilities and Joys. Parenting book for teenage fathers.

DO I HAVE A DADDY? A Story for a Single Parent Child. Also available in Spanish—*¿Yo tengo papá?*

DETOUR FOR EMMY. TOO SOON FOR JEFF. Novels about teenage pregnancy by Marilyn Reynolds.

TEENS PARENTING—Your Pregnancy and Newborn Journey. Prenatal health book for pregnant teens. Available in "regular" (RL 6), Easier Reading (RL 3), and Spanish (*Adolescentes como padres—la jornada de tu embarazo y el nacimiento de tu bebé*).

TEENS PARENTING—Your Baby's First Year. TEENS PARENTING—The Challenge of Toddlers. TEENS PARENTING—Discipline from Birth to Three. Three how-to-parent books for teenage parents.

BREAKING FREE FROM PARTNER ABUSE by Mary Marecek. Book for victims of domestic violence.

TEENAGE COUPLES—Caring, Commitment and Change; TEENAGE COUPLES—Coping with Reality. Two-book series gives teenagers a picture of the realities of marriage and living together.

TEENAGE COUPLES—Rainbows, Roles and Reality. A statistical comparison of teens' expectations of marriage with the realities of those already married or living together. 1995 publication.

SCHOOL-AGE PARENTS: The Challenge of Three-Generation Living. Help in dealing with the frustrations, problems, and pleasures of three-generation living.

TEEN PREGNANCY CHALLENGE, Book One: Strategies for Change; Book Two: Programs for Kids. Book One provides practical guidelines for developing adolescent pregnancy prevention and care programs. *Book Two* focuses on programs all along the adolescent pregnancy prevention continuum.

Please see ordering information on back of page.

MORNING GLORY PRESS

6595 San Haroldo Way, Buena Park, CA 90620-3748
714/828-1998 — FAX 714/828-2049

Please send the following:	Price	Total
Did My First Mother Love Me?		
_____ Paper, ISBN 0-930934-84-9	5.95	_____
_____ Cloth, ISBN 0-930934-85-7	12.95	_____
Open Adoption: A Caring Option		
_____ Paper, ISBN 0-930934-23-7	9.95	_____
Pregnant Too Soon: Adoption Is an Option		
_____ Paper, ISBN 0-930934-25-3	9.95	_____
Parents, Pregnant Teens and Adoption Option		
_____ Paper, ISBN 0-930934-28-8	8.95	_____
Adoption Awareness		
_____ Paper, ISBN 0-930934-32-6	12.95	_____
Surviving Teen Pregnancy		
_____ Paper, ISBN 0-930934-47-4	9.95	_____
Teen Dads		
_____ Paper, ISBN 0-930934-78-4	9.95	_____
_____ Cloth, ISBN 0-930934-77-6	15.95	_____
Do I Have a Daddy?		
_____ Paper, ISBN 0-930934-44-x	5.95	_____
_____ Cloth, ISBN 930934-45-8	12.95	_____
¿Yo tengo papá?		
_____ Paper, ISBN 0-930934-82-2	5.95	_____
_____ Cloth, ISBN 0-930934-83-0	12.95	_____
Detour for Emmy		
_____ Paper, ISBN 0-930934-76-8	8.95	_____
_____ Cloth, ISBN 0-930934-75-x	15.95	_____
Too Soon for Jeff		
_____ Paper, ISBN 0-930934-91-1	8.95	_____
_____ Cloth, ISBN 0-930934-90-3	15.95	_____
Breaking Free from Partner Abuse		
_____ Paper, ISBN 0-930934-74-1	7.95	_____
School-Age Parents: Three-Generation Living		
_____ Paper, ISBN 0-930934-36-9	10.95	_____

	Price	Total
Teens Parenting—Your Pregnancy and Newborn Journey		
_____ Paper, ISBN 0-930934-50-4	9.95	_____
Easier Reading Edition—*Your Pregnancy and Newborn Journey*		
_____ Paper, ISBN 0-930934-61-x	9.95	_____
Spanish—**Adolescentes como padres—La jornada de tu embarazo y el nacimiento de tu bebé**		
_____ Paper, ISBN 0-930934-69-5	9.95	_____
Teens Parenting—Your Baby's First Year		
_____ Paper, ISBN 0-930934-52-0	9.95	_____
Teens Parenting—Challenge of Toddlers		
_____ Paper, ISBN 0-930934-58-x	9.95	_____
Teens Parenting—Discipline from Birth to Three		
_____ Paper, ISBN 0-930934-54-7	9.95	_____
Teen Pregnancy Challenge:		
_____ *Bk. 1: Strategies for Change*	14.95	_____
_____ *Bk. 2: Programs for Kids*	14.95	_____
Teenage Couples: Caring, Commitment, Change		
_____ Paper, ISBN 0-930934-93-8	9.95	_____
_____ Cloth, ISBN 0-930934-92-x	15.95	_____
Teenage Couples: Coping with Reality		
_____ Paper, ISBN 0-930934-86-5	9.95	_____
_____ Cloth, ISBN 0-930934-87-3	15.95	_____
Teenage Couples: Rainbows, Roles and Reality		
_____ ISBN 0-930934-95-4 —1995 pub. PNS.		
TOTAL		_____
Please add postage: 10% of total—Min., $2.50		_____
California residents add 7.75% sales tax		_____
TOTAL		_____

Ask about quantity discounts, Workbooks, Teacher Guides. Prepayment requested.
School/library purchase orders accepted. If not satisfied, return in 15 days for refund.